Hailey

at Foxels Academy

Edition I

Hailey

at Foxels Academy

Edition I

Gaurika Joshi

ZORBA BOOKS

ZORBA BOOKS

Published by Zorba Books, October 2021

Website: www.zorbabooks.com
Email:info@zorbabooks.com

Author Name & Copyright © **Gaurika Joshi**
Title :- **Hailey at Foxels Academy: Edition I**

Printbook ISBN :- 978-93-90640-22-5
Ebook ISBN :- 978-93-90640-30-0

Zorba Books Pvt. Ltd. (opc)
Sushant Arcade,
Next to Courtyard Marriot,
Sushant Lok 1, Gurgaon — 122009, India

INDEX

Acknowledgments

Today when I am about to publish my maiden novel, I would like to thank the almighty God for giving me the strength and ability to do so.

I could write this novel during the tough time of pandemic due to the constant motivation of my parents. They would encourage and guide me always. I am what I am because of the values they taught me. My Dad helped me with the editing of the book in its initial phase, despite his busy office schedule.

My sincere thanks also to all family members, cousins, and extended members of the family.

I extend a special thanks to my sweet maternal Grandfather and Grandmother, Mr. Bhuwan Chandra Pant and Ms. Shanti Pant, whose inimitable sweetness, aura, and presence were indeed a blessing for a young child like me.

On this occasion, as I pen down my thoughts, I really miss my Grandparents, Mr. Suresh Chandra Joshi, and Ms. Prabha Joshi who are no more. I dedicate this novel to them.

I would like to place my sincere thanks to Shiv Nadar School, Gurgaon, India where I am presently studying. Principal Ma'am Ms. Monica would always inspire us to excel.

The wonderful teachers of my school had a terrific impact on me and always kept my mind ignited. My school teachers deserve the sincerest appreciation. This humble attempt to write the novel, the language, and the vocabulary, that I have acquired is because of my teachers.

I would also thank Zorba Books, who have been associated with the publishing part and providing creative inputs wherever necessary. I look forward to an even more fruitful association with them for my next edition.

The COVID 19 first and second wave wreaked havoc affecting each and every individual across the globe. We were also affected. Despite the problems, we decided to fight COVID-related challenges head-on. All three of us emerged victorious. We are safe and healthy now. Although the process of publishing got impacted, I do not have regrets. Life has taught me to handle challenges and face them with courage. Thanks to the almighty God for all his blessings.

Before signing off, I wish each one of YOU a fantastic NEW YEAR. May the year ahead always find you in the pink of Health and Happiness.

Stay Safe. Stay Healthy.

Prologue

Gaurika is a cherubic 12-year-old girl. Always full of energy with a passion to explore new subjects and excel in them. The world of magic always inspired and kept her mind ignited. She wanted to write a fiction-based novel on magic. She was only ten years old when she completed writing this novel. We could feel the unflinching determination and sparkle in her eyes when Gaurika said "Mom and Dad. I want to write a novel on magic". She was nine years old then.

We were under the impression that like any other child she must have said that in a playful mood. Time flew by. The world was affected by COVID. Despite the challenges, the resolve of a nine-year child and the novelist in her did not wither down. She would keep her mind ignited and quietly keep jotting down ideas for her maiden novel.

Then one fine day when she was about ten years old, Gaurika said "Mom and Dad I have completed writing the novel". We could not believe it. After going through the pages, it was indeed a pleasant surprise for us. What unfurled was the creativity of a nine-year-old child which gradually matured over a period of time into an interesting novel.

We could see a writer in Gaurika. What follows is the First edition. The content is purely imaginative and fiction-based. Finding a publisher was the next challenging task. After considerable effort and time, we could zero in on Zorba publishers, who helped Gaurika in the publishing process. The first edition is purely Gaurika's own efforts and imagination. Also, a reflection of a talented writer in times to come.

All the best Gaurika.

God bless you

Mom and Dad

An Unknown Letter

It was a bright Monday morning. A perfect week day for school in the Seattle city of Washington DC.

"Hailey! Hurry my child or else you will get late for school! The bus will arrive in five minutes from now!!!``said Jenny Hailey's mom.

"Coming mom coming. I am just wearing my shoes!!!"

"Uh stop making so much noise you two", said Uncle Steve. "Can't you see I am sleeping? It is early morning and you are creating such a ruckus!! Stop this cacophony and go downstairs".

"Ok uncle", said Hailey.

"Uh it is so boring to go to school after the winter holidays. And today is the last day to give all the gifts muttered Hailey to herself.

"You have finally come down." Said Hailey's mother Miss Jenny Malicia.

"Yes I did", said Hailey with a frown.

"What happened, why are you frowning?"

"It's just that everybody got something from their Secret Santa except for me."

"Oh that's fine but what exactly happens in that Secret Santa?" she enquired inquisitively.

"Well, a lot of slips of paper are put in a decorated Christmas box with each slip of paper containing the names of all my classmates. For supposing if I pick up a slip and get the name of a child whose name is Scarlet, I am supposed to give gifts to Scarlet, but I have to do so secretly. This game ends after the winter break. After the winter break we sit down in a circle and disclose whose Secret Santa were we. Unfortunately, my Secret Santa has not given me any gifts."

"That's alright Hailey, maybe you get an extra-ordinary gift today."

"Well, let me hope for the best", said Hailey and left for the bus stop.

"Oh hi Hailey how nice to see you!!" said Scarlet, a sassy classmate of Hailey.

"Nice to see you too Scarlet. Are you excited to meet your friends again?" Said Hailey.

"Oh yes of course. Isn't it so obvious everybody is really excited about meeting their friends again? By the way did you check your Christmas mail box maybe you got something from your Secret Santa.....because my Secret Santa has given me so many things like a card and a....."

"Oh no I almost forgot to check my Christmas mailbox, I gotta go.....right away, bye!!" said Hailey interrupting Scarlet.

When she opened the Christmas mailbox she saw a letter and was shocked because no one had ever given her any letter!! Now the way she felt was somewhat like this:

"What.... I got a letter. I wonder what message it would

have for me. Who would want to message me!! I am not so special to anyone... except maybe my Secret Santa wrote it for me and maybe it describes me. Hmm let's see..."

"Oh my god! This is so awesome and, well, a little terrific. Is this school real? Is magic real? Is any of this real? Or I am just dreaming. She was so excited. She wanted to go to that school today!! I can't believe I am invited to a *MAGICAL* school.

OH MY GOD

OH MY GOD

OH MY GOD!" said Hailey in the madness of extreme happiness

Along with this swell of excitement, many other things were going on in her mind. After all, the envelope was clipped with a hat that looked scary, cool and magical, but also absurd. The letter was written in the world's most beautiful handwriting ever!!!!

A lot was going on.....

"I have to go home and show this to my mom and sister and brother and..... everybody, but I need to go home for that. Of - course! I should ask the guard. I bet he will allow me.

Umm excuse me guard uncle can you allow me to go home? Please, this is very important."

"I am sorry Hailey but the gates are closed. You have to go when school is over." Replied the guard.

"But I have a letter to give. Can you please make an exception?"

The guard thought for some while, looked at his wristwatch twice, and then said to Hailey who was about to faint if he would have said a no.

"Ok since I've known you for about six years, so I guess I will make an exception from the principal."

Thank you, very much guard uncle, this is an unpayable favor of yours."

"Ok now off you go", said the guard.

When she reached her house her mom was shocked because she had come back from school in just 20 minutes. When her mother asked why she did so, Hailey said "Mum look, I got an amazing letter from another school of magic. Can you believe it!!!"

"Well no I can't", said mum "and give that letter right away you girl."

After reading the letter she couldn't believe herself, SHE WAS SHOCKED. Once she read the letter she said "What!!! This is so crazy. There is no way I am sending you there. Who knows how safe this school is. Plus I don't want anything to happen to you. You are the only thing I..."

"Oh shut up mom, don't emotionally blackmail."

"Yeah, I mean, you don't even care." Said mum.

"But mom, look there are other people out there who are completely safe and the school invited me because I am meant to be there.

You can't just say no like that, you have to send me and I promise I will be completely safe no matter what."

"Fine, I shall allow you but you will come back safe, alright?"

"Alright, mum alright."

"So now are you waiting for Christmas or what? Go to your room and start packing. Come on quick. You have a train to catch tomorrow.

Journey To Foxels

"Wake up Hailey!! You don't want to miss the train".

"Oh mum, have a look at least, your girl is ready. I just can't find my letter. Please help me find the letter as it contains the platform's name and other important details for reaching Foxels academy."

"Well I kept it in your regular school bag", mum said.

"Oh, that is pretty nice of you". Said Hailey sarcastically.

"It's called being ready." Said Hailey's mum.

"Mom, should we stop our conversation now, and rush to the train station or will you wait for me to miss the train?" said Hailey.

"Ok let's go, come on." Replied her mum.

"Yes! We finally reached it. I can't believe it took us one whole hour to reach the train station." Said Hailey trying to wake her mom who had fallen asleep on

route to the station from her house.

"We reached!" said mum, yawning and waking up from her deep sleep. "I thought it would be difficult even to reach the train station, forget about the school"

"Uh, mom get over it please."

"Ok fine but anyway where is your dear Platform Alfa Century 2340?" asked mum.

"Umm I don't know, but the guard must know." Replied Hailey.

"And where is the guard exactly?" asked her mom.

"Right over there mom. I will go ask other people about the platform. So, you go and ask the guard and till then I will ask the other people about the Platform, ok?"

"Ok sweetheart." Replied Hailey's mom.

While Hailey's mom asked the guard, Hailey found the Tilt family.

"Hey!! Excuse me, do you guys know about Platform Alfa Century 2340?"

"Oh so you are also from FOXELS ACADEMY?" said Melina Tilt, a young girl.

"Technically not yet, but I am going there for the first time."

"Oh, well my name is Melina Tilt and my younger brother James Tilt over here is also going for the first time, but I have another brother..."

"Hailey, where are you?" Texted Hailey's mum.

"Mom, meet me next to the pole," texted Hailey. "I think I found the Platform."

"Ok sweetheart coming."

"Yes Melina continue please", said Hailey looking at a

pole with a hat drawn on it curiously. The hat drawn on it was black and had a blood-red stripe on it. About the pole, well it was pretty different and distinct in its appearance because it didn't have blocks dividing it, in fact, it was puzzlingly plain. Hailey wasn't sure whether the pole was clear cement in fact she thought it was clay!!!!!

"Yeah, so before I tell you anything let me tell you two things. One, that I am attending my fifth year in Foxels. And two, that pole is made up of clay, in case you were wondering." Said Melina.

With the air of confusion removed now, Hailey knew that the pole was made of clay.

"I have other brothers who are also in the school. If you are finding Platform Alfa Century 2340, say 'Open up K Davara' and then you will see that conical hat flying towards your face, and whoosh you will be sucked inside like a vacuum cleaner" said Melina. "Well, just see how my elder brother Dave goes inside the hat", exclaimed Melina.

"Uh ok but just wait I will call mom. She can't find me at all" said Hailey.

"Yeah, ok-ok I'll wait."

"Mom, where are you?"

Texted Hailey.

"I can see you. Can't you see me?" Replied Hailey's Mom.

By the time Hailey took a glance around, to see her mother, Melina said "Is she your mother?"

Hailey took one look and recognized her mother.

"What took you so long" Said Hailey to her mother.

"Oh nothing, just got lost. Though is it true you found the platform?" Replied her mum.

"Yeah! Come along let me show you." Replied Hailey

And as explained by Hailey they went to the pole, which was the entry to Platform Alfa Century 2340.

"Oh hey Hailey is this your mum." quipped Melina.

"Yes." Replied Hailey.

"And who is she?" asked Hailey's mum.

"She is Melina Tilt" answered Hailey.

"Oh so is she the girl who told you about the Platform?"

"Yes mum, she is the girl."

"Ok, so where is Platform Alfa Century 2340?"

"So, Hailey has to say Open up k Davara, and then go through that pole." Said Melina.

"No way I letting her bump her head like that!!" Rued Hailey's mum.

No Ma'am... trust me... nothing is gonna happen.. it's fine and gonna be ok... if you don't trust me, lemme show it to you. Just a second....said Melina pointing out towards Dave.

Dave!!! Don't you want to go to Foxels? C'mon....say the chant and go to the platform."

"Ok sis", said Dave answering Melina.

And lo behold!!! As soon as Dave spelled out the magical chant, the hat flew towards him, absorbed him like a vacuum absorbs dust, and Bingo!!! He disappeared before

Hailey's mum. She could couldn't comprehend what had happened.

"Wow, that was... well unbelievable!" said mum in utter disbelief. Even though she was now secure about the fact that Hailey would be safe doing all this, she was stubborn to admit it.

"Mom, now can I try saying the chant, go swirling right into the hat and finally reach the Platform Alfa Century?" Asked Hailey.

"Ok Hailey bye, see you then."

"Bye", said Hailey.

And without holding up her excitement any further she spelled out the magical spell *Open up k davara*........

The moment she muttered out the chant, Hailey got sucked up by the hat just as if pulled by a powerful whirlpool and reached Platform Alfa Century 2340.

"Oh my god, I finally reached. I mean I still can't believe magic is real.. well anyways the train is about to leave and I should probably just rush " said Hailey

"Everybody board the train!!!" Shouted the guard. Everybody started boarding the train and Hailey was pleasantly surprised at yet another coincidence to find a seat beside James Tilt. They both started talking after some time.

"Hey you are Hailey Mailsa something," said James.

"MALICIA!!!" corrected Hailey visibly irritated as she had a penchant for remembering names when introduced. Friends and teachers always appreciated her for this. **"HAILEY MALICIA,"** said Hailey, ensuring that James would now remember her name.

"Yeah, fine Hailey something, listen to me since you have never been to this school and I know about every single corner of this school. How would you like it if I would be your guide for the year," said James.

"Umm well........No thanks I think I can ask my teachers and I do not think they will hesitate in telling me the way to my classes for sure." quipped Hailey.

"First of all, they are not teachers, they are professors," said James.

"Ok, I got it smarty pants. You can tell me whatever you want to tell me, but I will still do what I want to do," replied Hailey.

"Oh can you both just shut up so I can read a book." said an unknown girl sounding visibly irritated.

The two of them glanced at each other and started giggling.

When the two of them finally stopped, the unknown girl asked "Can I please know why were you laughing like stupid witches and wizards?"

"We weren't laughing like stupid witches or wizards it's just that you have orange paint on your nose, and you look hilarious," said James.

"Well it's nothing to laugh so much about, dumb heads." said the unknown girl.

"Stop shouting you all," said an irritated voice of a lady with a fat face, thick body, and a barely visible neck.

"This is a train, and I personally didn't think Kyle would be making such a ruckus" repeated the lady.

"You are right. I would never ever do such a thing but these dumb heads wouldn't listen I was just trying to read, but when they started making so much noise I was very disturbed. So I went to their place and then we started arguing." said Kyle (the unknown girl was Kyle).

"Do a Deal Do a Deal" said the fat lady.

"What again?" asked Hailey aloud.

"It means to be friends for a session and curse yourself to forget each other forever if you find your relationship bad, but if not then you continue with it," said Kyle.

"So what do you think about it," said the fat lady?

"Well I don't mind a try," said James.

"I don't mind it either", said Kyle.

"I really don't know. It seems kind of harsh," said Hailey.

"Oh don't worry, it isn't as harsh as it seems, nobody has really ever cursed themselves. The group always became friends." Said the fat lady Ms. Harshly Hearts, reassuring Hailey.

"Ok, maybe there is no harm in trying", said Hailey.

"Time to get off", shouted the guard.

"Come now time to get off the train. Come on quick, oh...and take care", said Mrs. Harshly Hearts.

The three kids hugged Mrs. Heart and went off.

Welcome To Foxels

The moment they stepped on the ground they saw a ginormous tower named

"Welcome to Foxels" A lot of whispering started to happen when a tall, slim lady came through the hall. She was wearing a black gown.

"My name is Midnight Mowlem and I am the Deputy Head Mistress of this school. This tower's name as you can see is Welcome to Foxels. It is ten thousand feet long and this tower is special because no human can see it and if they somehow see it they can't enter it because of strong entry barriers compounded with the highest level of security. When you go up with me on each floor to buy all your things using the elevator and reach the last floor, you have to jump without saying a single word. After you jump you enter the school and you wait for the whole class and me. Any questions?"

"Yes," said Hailey. "How will we buy the stuff if we don't have money and how much time will it take to buy all this and what if we get hurt while we jump... after all, it is ten thousand feet long and how do you know it is safe and......."

"Too many questions at once. Sorry, but none can be answered, and about the money all the equipment is free for now."

"What do you mean free for now?" asked James.

"When you grow up all the money you earn will be deposited to your lockers and you will pay then. The only reason you don't pay now is because your lockers are empty. Once they are full you shall pay. Now no time to waste, let's move on." And so as they moved on they went through the elevator. The first floor read **_"Wizardry and witchcraft clothes"_**

The shop looked pretty old and rusty, though everybody seemed to like it a lot.

"This shop is for your clothes, you shall buy your clothes, choose them, try them out in ten minutes and no talking, girls and boys this is individual work so I don't want a sound. Ok so now we will just go in proper groups of girls and boys. GIRLS! Hurry Up!! Go and do as I say and remember, not a single word now!!! Come on go quick hurry up." And off went all the girls in the shop.

"Which color will you take" asked Kyle to Hailey very politely.

"We can choose a color!!! I don't even know what colors there are .... I don't know anything", said Hailey.

"Oh well, you soon will know what means what. Maybe you could ask Miss Maria or Miss Marina. They know everything about Foxels."

Hailey barely knew anything about the teachers and her mind was filled up with a lot of probing questions as she was mesmerized with the experience till now, but she still went to the teachers full of curiosity to know about the uniform.

"Um Miss Marina could you tell me about the school uniforms, you see I don't really know anything about what to take, which color to pick up? I am having some problems, so could you help?"

"Why not!! Of course, I will. Isn't that what teachers are for?" said Ms. Marina, one of the teachers.

"Oh err um sorry"

"It's okay dear what was your question again? Oh yes, you were asking me about what you have to wear isn't that so?"

"Yes."

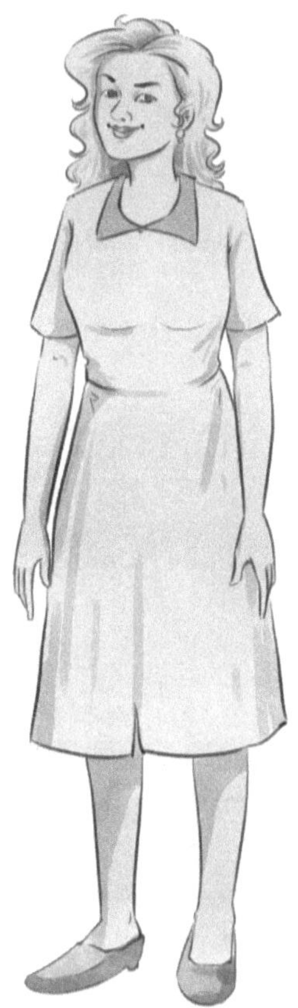

Ms Marina Gave Hailey the clothes. Hailey got all dressed up.

"Well for now these are the clothes you will need." Said Ms. Marina.

Oh!! Ok now I get it and I love the type of clothes and their color is gorgeous I JUST LOVE THEM!!! Said Hailey.

Great!! So should I pack this set for you? Said Marina.

"Yes, Miss Marina!"

After some time Hailey knew a lot about Foxels Academy. After all, they had gone through a ten thousand feet long tower and it was not a small deal. Every shopkeeper told her more and more about the academy and as mentioned, now she knew a lot about Foxels Academy, in fact, she thought she knew her new enchanted school of magic even better than James!

Now came the part from which everyone feared, Yes

Friends!!! It was the part in which every single student had to jump down without any sort of tantrums. Especially with a professor like Midnight Mowlem. She was seriously the strictest professor Hailey knew about, till now! She wouldn't allow tantrums, wouldn't tell another way to the castle, and worst of all, even though she could have used the easy way via her magic, Professor Mowlem, a known stickler of rules, would not relent. She wanted the students to jump from a ginormous height of ten thousand feet without uttering a single word to gain an entry into Foxels Academy. One had to agree, she was one real up-tight lady with a lot of **POWER!!!**

She was literally limitless, but anyways there was no point in talking about this matter. She wasn't going to let us do the fun stuff. Anyways, now it was Hailey's turn to jump!!

THREE......TWO... ONE......AND......GO!!!!!!!!!!!!!!!!!!

WOAH!!!

And right into the academy did Hailey reach!

It was the biggest miracle of her life! It just happened in a fraction of a second.

When she was over with her illusions she saw that there were many other people around her. She saw everyone except professor Midnight Mowlem. She felt a bit insecure and......

Miss Mowlem fell down with BOOM!!!

"OUCH!"

"HAILEY ARE YOU A MAD GIRL OR WHAT?

ONCE YOU ENTER THE ACADEMY YOU ARE SUPPOSED TO GET UP AND STAND IN THE LINE LIKE

EVERY SINGLE STUDENT IS. YOU WOULD HAVE BEEN IN BIG TROUBLE IF THIS WASN'T YOUR FIRST DAY!!!"

"Sorry Professor Mowlem, won't ever happen again," said Hailey apologetically.

"Better be!!"

Besties Forever

It was the second day of school and Kyle was so excited that she went to Hailey's room, dragged her from her bed, and wiggled her as fast as possible!!! Hailey did not like this behavior. Hailey's barometer of anger shot up for this action of Kyle. She wanted to shout at her, but she didn't, because she remembered that she had promised to keep the "do a deal do a deal" and according to that, all of the things were *BANNED!!!*

But anyway she just woke up (not that she had a choice!) and...

◎ Brushed her teeth

◎ Washed her face with soap

◎ Took a cool refreshing bath with icy water (since it is very hot in there)

◎ Ironed her clothes

◎ Wore them on

◎ Fixed her messy bed

◎ Combed her hair

◎ Put a fancy hairband

- ◎ Wore Sox which had a very thin cloth
- ◎ Polished her blood-red shoes and made them pretty shiny
- ◎ Wore the shoes on
- ◎ And went with Kyle

"Morning children!!!" said Miss Harshly Hearts.

"MISS HARSHLY HEARTS!!! Said the two of them, surprised.

But we thought you would go back to your house when you had dropped us off at Foxels!"

"Oh!! If I go you would starve to death!!!" Said Ms. Hearts.

"**WHAT?**" Said Hailey and Kyle.

"Yes kids, I am the cook of this academy. It was just yesterday that I was on the bus too. You see, my sister was on leave so I did the job for her." Replied Ms. Hearts.

TRRRRRR! Rang the bell as loud as a lion's roar!

"Ah, there we go. Come on children time to go to the Assembly room" said Ms. Hearts.

"Is it necessary to go?" I mean who wants to see the face of the strictest teacher in the whole of Foxels remarked Hailey

"Well Mowlem is not the only professor you see, there are other professors. Do you know that today you are going to know everyone, everything and every subject!! So I suggest that you should probably go." said

Ms. Harshly.

"Ok, I don't mind. And anyway I have come here to learn," said Hailey.

"Then off you go," said Ms. Harshly.

When they reached the assembly area they saw Mowlem and also noticed that all the other teachers were also standing out there. As they watched, Mowlem started her speech-

"Good morning everyone, today you will know everything about this school. To know about the information read the information board. For any queries be free to ask the Headmaster of Our school Tentus Organio."

<u>**Subjects-**</u>

<u>**Defending using Magic**</u>

<u>**Attacking using Magic**</u>

<u>**Transformation using magic**</u>

<u>**Advance Magic Tricks**</u>

<u>**Invincible Power using magic**</u>

<u>**Teachers and Their Subjects**</u>

<u>**Tentus Organio -**</u> **Headmaster**

<u>**Midnight Mowlem -**</u> **Professor of Teaching Defense from Magic**

<u>**Phelix Tribly -**</u> **Professor of Teaching Attack from Magic**

<u>**Mejia Forkite -**</u> **Professor Teaching Transformation**

<u>**Dentin Olas -**</u> **Professor of Teaching Advance Magic Tricks**

<u>**Tender Miles -**</u> **Professor of Teaching Invincible Power**

<u>**Octavius Contagion -**</u> **Professor of Teaching Human Studies**

This is the map of Foxels. Foxels Academy is surrounded by a red color light that makes it invisible for ordinary people.

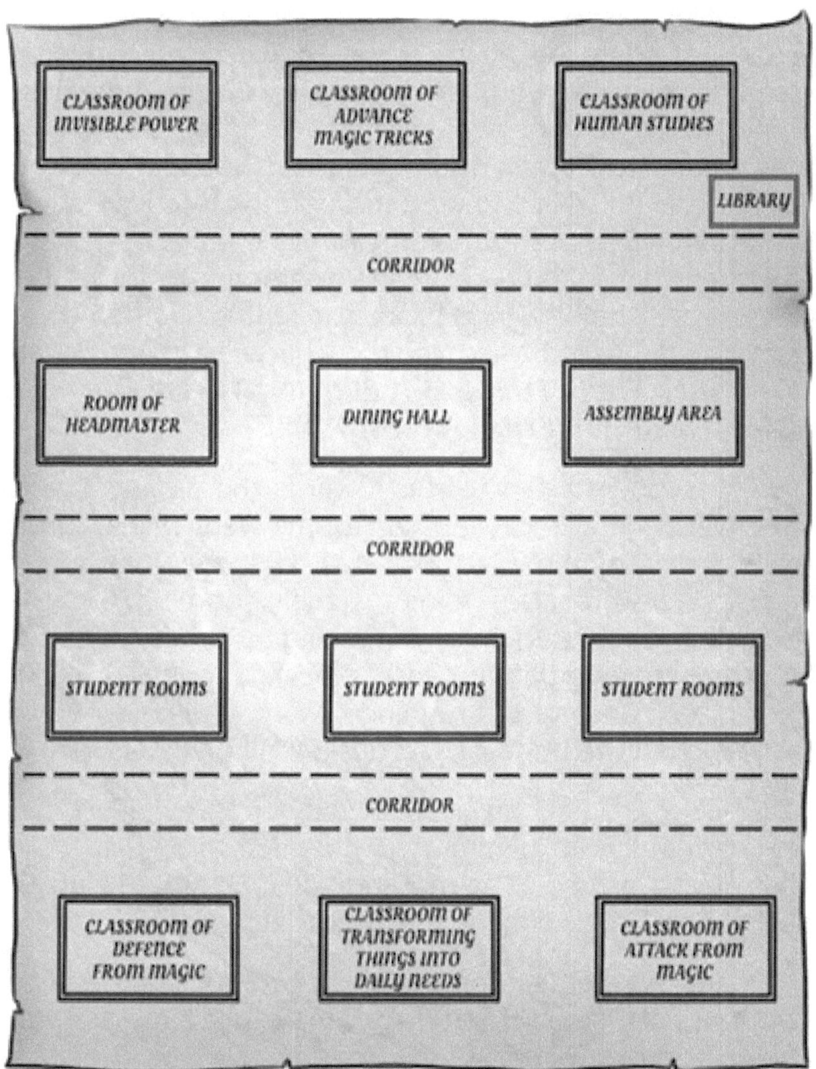

The narrative by Mowlem set the excitement buzzing amongst the first years. They were thrilled and spell-bound during the acclimatization process with the professors, their magical expertise, the classrooms, and what was in store for them.

Hjfgg c acbnbc....were the buzzing sounds of the first years that could be heard along the corridors when the assembly was over and they were escorting toward the dining hall. Everyone was excited for their classes when they heard the scared voice of Miss Harshly Heart could be heard from a distance tearing through the buzzing sounds. Ms. Harshly was seen running along the corridor. She was so scared that it looked as if she was going to forget how to even breathe!!!!! When Professor Tentus Organio a very calm person, asked Miss Harshly what was going on, she said ***"FIRE...FIRE...THERE IS A FIRE IN THE LIBRARY...DO SOMETHING IMMEDIATELY...HURRY!!"***

Everyone started to run towards the assembly area. They went there because their rooms were placed under the grounds of the assembly area. Like everyone, Hailey and James were also going to their rooms when they remembered that their most intelligent friend Kyle was labeling her new books in the library. They took a turn and a deep breath and started running towards the library. When they reached there they saw a bucket full of water.

"HELP HELP" they heard Kyle shouting... Please help me. I am stuck in this library which is in fire "help-help". There was no time to waste and so James picked up the bucket and Hailey pitched in by giving the water.

After some time, everything was cool. Kyle felt very safe now and said "I am so grateful. I can't express my gratitude toward you two for saving my life."

"It's fine. Anyway, 's we have made a promise to be friends," said Hailey

"Yeah," said James.

"Well not to be the negative one but all my books got burnt in fire." Said Kyle.

"Kyle!!" Said Hailey and James.

They were so engrossed in talking that they didn't notice that the whole of Foxels had gathered and so had the Professors. The Headmaster then said "we are proud of the manner you have handled the situation with spontaneity. But you are not supposed to be hanging out in the fire alone!!!!!"

"He is right, you know," said Mowlem in a humble voice.

"But how could we leave her alone, Kyle is my friend," said Hailey.

"What?" said Kyle in shock!!

"Yes. All that time you've been with me. I liked you even though we had our differences. You were like my best friend!!" said Hailey

The professors looked at one another, smiled, and left the corridor.

After that day the three of them were very-very-very close friends. They would share almost everything with each other from small school matters to very big secrets. They were besties forever!!!!

Pet Selection

It was after some time that the first years were called to the assembly area again. Everyone had to go because usually very important announcements were made there. Once everybody had gathered in the assembly area, Miss Forkite the sweetest, respected, loved and the most pretty professor started her speech saying -

"Good Morning one and all. You must be thinking about why we gathered in a place like an assembly area. Well here is the answer to this. We gathered here to tell you that today and tomorrow, May 01-02 have been earmarked for pet selection. "We will be having a pet selection! In the pet selection, names will be called out and you will choose either Unicorn or Alicorn or Pegasus or Pony. It is necessary for each student to choose a pet. Once they name their pet, they will fill a form the next day in which they will write the name of their pet. Once this action of finalizing is done it can't be undone. Thank you."

"Yay!!" said the big crowd of students to miss Forkite.

"This activity begins NOW."

"Kyle Stone," said Forkite.

"I choose a unicorn." Said Kyle "

"Good choice," said Forkite.

"Charlie Hoopster" shouted Forkite.

"I choose a pony" said Charlie

"Nice one Charlie." Replied Forkite.

"Alishia Miller" shouted Forkite again.

"I choose a Pegasus," said Alishia.

"Wintin Linto," said Forkite.

"I choose an Alicorn," said Wintin.

"James Tilt" Forkite yelled out loud.

"I chose a pony! And I want his name to be" said James

"Calm down little one. Names have to be selected tomorrow!!!!" said Forkite chuckling.

"Oh!! Ok" replied James and went off.

"Hailey Malicious" yelled Forkite again.

"I choose an Alicorn!!" Said Hailey.

"Wonderful choice there!" Replied Forkite

"Losete Noloness" Forkite called out.

"Unlike other DUMBS miss Forkite I chose a pony" Said Losete.

"Ok" Replied Forkite.

Every first-year got a chance to select their pet, but James, Kyle and Hailey hated the way Losete had behaved. She was a good witch but shouldn't have called everyone else dumb!!!

While they were walking their way back to their rooms they met Losete and the moment they saw her they knew that their day would be bad after that. As expected Losete went to the trio and started mocking them.

"Hey losers.

I mean what dumbs you are.

Kyle is so pathetic and lame. What a nerd. And the boy you should stop acting like a know it all, because even you know that you are nothing but a dumb head.

And the last one, you are invited to Foxels, but don't even know anything about Foxels. Huh, I can't believe Foxels has really invited you."

"At least we have a proper family. Your mother and father are in Seastus jail for their severe crimes. " said Hailey.

Losete was speechless. She ran to her room sobbing.

Her parents were criminals. They had committed several murders and crimes. Losete lived with her grandma, as her parents were usually in jail.

Tomorrow morning was a very big day for the students. There was a bulge of excitement because today the students had to name their pets!!!

Everyone made a HUGE line in the assembly area. Everybody was called inside this very small room privately in which they were told to fill the form and finalize their pet's name. One professor stood out and one professor stood in to control the students. As usual Hailey, James and Kyle stood together and Kyle was the next one to go in. This is how the conversation went like-

"Miss Mowlem, could I get the form?"

"Yes.... Here you go"

"Thanks."

NAME- Kyle Stone

AGE- 11

ROOM NUMBER- 203

YEAR IN SCHOOL- Year 1

MOTHER'S NAME- Ella Stone

FATHER'S NAME- Seastus Stone

PET KIND- Unicorn

PET NAME- Minismartia

FINALIZE-Minismartia

SIGNATURE-

"Done?" asked Mowlem.

"Yes Professor Mowlem." Replied Kyle.

"Good. Now you may take your pet." Said Mowlem.

"Really!!" asked Kyle in excitement.

"Do I lie?" replied Mowlem.

"No...... you...d...don't. S...sorry miss" said Kyle getting scared after hearing Mowlem's firm voice.

"Now go." said Mowlem firmly.

Pony, Pegasus, Unicorn, Alicorn Game Tournament

The next day the children's first class was tournament prep. Miss Hepburn came down in her sports attire with shorts. Her students also followed in with shorts and a shirt. As they started their class Hepburn told them to sit on their pets. Then she told them to hit their pet for moving on.

She showed an example with her pet Fifi. She was Pegasus and she was very obedient indeed. This is how it went like:

As Hepburn hit Fifi with her hand and said go, Fifi flew into the air along with Hepburn. When Hepburn told her pet to go right, Fifi would go right, when Hepburn told Fifi to go left, Fifi would go left. Fifi would follow every single command of Hepburn who had a stupendous control on Fifi. Fifi would take turns as swift as a Ferrari in full throttle and lightning speed. No matter how sharp or wiggly the turn was the pair would go across it and clear through the way and at last they did a landing so soft it didn't make a single sound. It was as quiet as a mouse trying to run out from a clowder.

After one month the tournament's first round began.

Everyone was prepared. Professor Dentin Olas started his speech by saying "hello children. I am Olas, Dentin Olas. I am happy to start this tournament and so it begins from now, before starting let me tell you the rules of this game.

1. One can only shoot a goal on his or her opponent's side .

2. If the girl or boy shoots on their own side, it will be a wizard's foul.

3. The foul will be costly because then the person who has done the wizard's foul that person's team will lose ten points.

4. If the team has a foul for the second time then the team loses thirty points.

5. If the foul repeats for the third time then the person's team will lose fifty points and the team will have one player out of the team."

Then Olas said the teams from a sheet of paper.

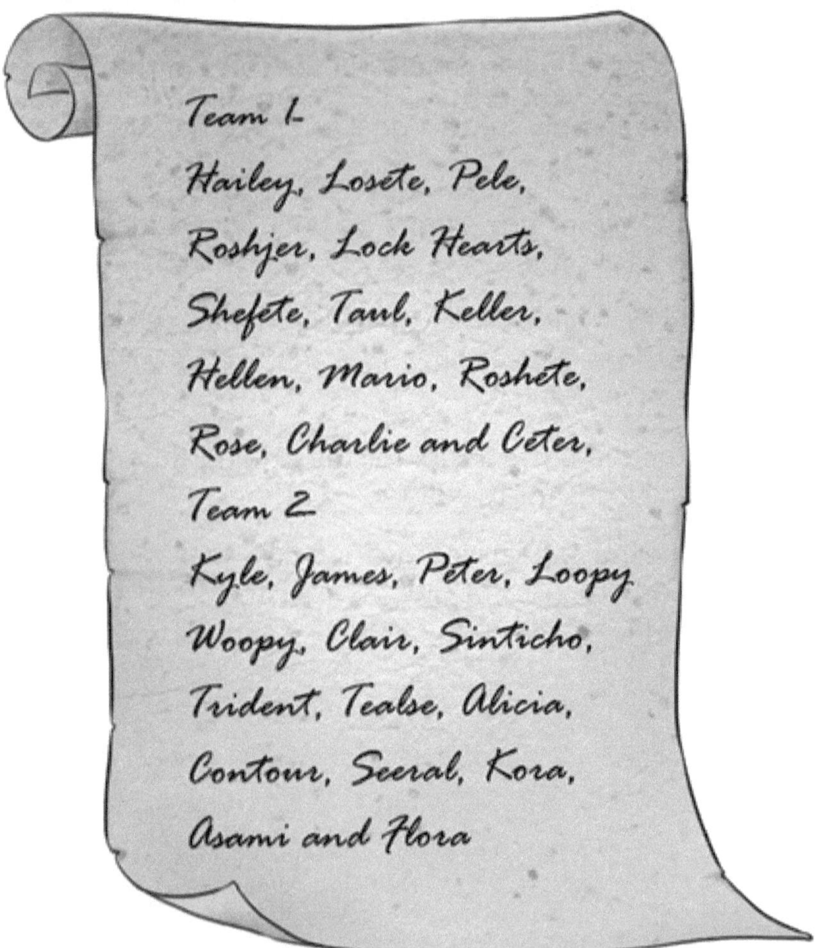

Forkite was the referee so she bounced the ball high up in the air and said "THE GAME BEGINS NOW!!!"

FWEET! Came the sound of the whistle and

So began the game!!

The tournament and competition were fierce and intense because Losete and Hailey were a very strong and powerful combination. Even though they had their own differences this one similarity made them a winning pair. This similarity did not exactly make them friends but by being and working together they were an invincible deterrent for any team competing against them.

Likewise Kyle's team was no less because her team had James, someone who had the control on his Pegasus so well that he had once defeated Hepburn, the biggest star seen till now. Another guy called Sinticho, also was a great flyer. He had once covered the whole school's boundary in just 6 seconds!! Now that was a record. His name was found in the school record book page 65 with the heading of the schools greatest and fastest flyers, line 13.

Kyle was actually not a great player because she was someone who was more of the smarty types, whereas Hailey, Losete, James and Sinticho were very sporty indeed.

Each team scored a point it was getting impossible to decide who was going to be the winning team. Each team had 40-40 points, until the round 10. The game seemed to be never ending hence Organio announced that this round would be the final round.

When the ball was tossed up in the air by Forkite the ball accidentally hit Sinticho's specs and his spec fell down and broke. When James told Sinticho to get a new pair of specs, Sinticho told them he would somehow manage. James agreed and continued.

When the ball came into the hands of Sinticho, James shouted and told Sinticho to pass the ball to James. As Sinticho could only see blur he erroneously passed the ball to Hailey who put a goal.

"And the winner is <u>The Eagles</u>" shouted the referee.

The Eagles team was actually Hailey's team. Hailey was so happy that she shouted loud enough to crack all the glasses present in the area. The other team, which was James' team, congratulated The Eagles and left.

That day was over and so was the utmost fierce match. That day was a very calm day. Not a single sound was being heard in the academy. The reason for such silence and tranquillity all over the academy was because everyone was tired. The ones who played were tired of playing. The ones who watched were tired of cheering. The referee was tired of telling rules, regulations, and scores. And lastly the professors were tired of sitting. They were tired of sitting because the seats that were in the game field were of very poor quality, and so their knees were as stiff as rocks. These issues had made the school tired and hence everyone was extremely silent. However, the school and the environment was never ever boring. There was something magical about it with every day adding a new colour and dimension to what the students were learning.

With each passing day teaching something new, the time had now come for the students to take their exams and impress their professors with the knowledge acquired from them. After two months came December the month which was in Foxels known as Santa's month because in December Christmas was celebrated. Unfortunately this Christmas something bad was going to happen......

Christmas Time

Christmas time was nearly there and everybody was very excited. **Poppy (Hailey's multi-talented Alicorn), Minismartia (Kyle's smart unicorn) and Inteligentiosaurus (James absurd named pony)** played all day and all night. The place was full of joy and laughter. Christmas was going to start tomorrow and it would end next week. In the magic world or at least at Foxels, Christmas is celebrated for 7 days.

One fine day, when the Christmas decorations were being put on the large halls of Foxels, every student was called to the assembly room. Everybody, as usual, was very curious and so they went to the assembly area. When they went to the assembly area they saw all the professors and employees standing there.

When the students entered the assembly hall, Organio started his speech by saying "Hello students. Merry Christmas. Christmas starts tomorrow and so we wanted to celebrate this wonderful occasion this year as usual, we wanted to celebrate it differently this time. We have decided to play a game. Ready Hailey?"

Everyone looked at Hailey so curiously that for a moment, Hailey felt like running away from the hall.

Hailey went on the stage and so she looked at her piece of paper and started saying "Well, a lot of slips of paper are put in a decorated Christmas box with each slip of paper containing the names of all my classmates. For supposing if I pick up a slip and get the name of a child whose name is Scarlet, I am supposed to give gifts to Scarlet, but I have to do so secretly. This game ends after the winter break. After the winter break we sit down in a circle and disclose whose Secret Santa were we."

Everyone **loved the game** a lot. They were all very excited to play. The chits would be distributed soon. Everybody was happy, but as usual there was one kid unhappy, 'Losete.'

Losete went to Hailey and said —

"Hey loser. Couldn't even keep your stupid non-magical game out of the magical world." Said Losete.

"First of all, stupid people think everything is stupid, and secondly; you need to learn to chill out Losete." Said Hailey.

"Uh, amateur witches like you are a shame to this world." Said Losete.

"Gee! Thanks for the compliment. Now I am used to it." Replied Hailey.

"I hate you!" Fired Losete.

"Back at you...thank you, bye." Replied Hailey and went away.

There was a tradition in Foxels academy. One day before Christmas, all students and professors students would gather near the monstrous sea and decorate the humongous magical tree near the sea. All schools did it, so it wasn't only a tradition in Foxels, but Foxels Academy always was the first one to put their decorations up every Christmas.

Then all schools would gather and sit down in a campfire, and students would interact with other students from other schools. Then they would gather in a circle and pray to the 7 Lords of magic. Out of which 4 Lords had passed away. Only Lord Reginald, Lord Ogminus and Lord Horehoof, were alive to take care of the magical word.

This tradition was **BEAUTIFUL**. Hailey was so excited she could barely breathe.

When the time arrived the festival started and it was lovely. All schools had gathered around. There were so many students! All schools had different mythical creatures to choose as pets. For example in Foxels it was – Unicorn, Alicorn, Pony or Pegasus, but in another academy called (Angels and Saints Academy for only wizards) it was Griffins, Owls or a Dragon. There were so many more academies, so there were so many pets that were there. Hailey met this boy called Lucas. He seemed familiar, as if they were connected or something.

This is how their conversation went:

"Hello there!" Said Hailey.

"Hola mi amigo! May I know your good name?" Replied Lucas.

"Ooh..... Spanish, I like it! My name is Hailey, Hailey Malicious. What's your name?" Fired Hailey.

"My name is Lucas, Lucas Madison. I am the grandson of, well, my grandpa who is what every magical being calls 'Lord Reginald.' Hailey, I have heard about you before. My friend James told me that you are a great girl and an amazing friend too, will you be my friend?" Said Lucas.

"Sure I would love a friend, but you gotta teach me Spanish." Replied Hailey.

"Done and Done!" Said Lucas.

The celebration was amazing. Students and professors from all schools prayed to the 7 Lords of magic. This was very special for Hailey as she did not only enjoy the celebration to the fullest, but she also made a new friend.

She was very excited for the next day, because tomorrow it would be Christmas time!

Secret Santa

The next morning was Christmas's first day. Everyone gathered in the assembly area to start the Secret Santa, and according to the instruction given by Hailey, they started picking up the slips. Everyone got names and few children even got names of professors!!

Excitement was buzzing in the air. Then Organio came and said "Gift Giving starts NOW!!!"

Hailey picked up her slip and she had gotten Losete. Was this done purposely??

She thought that this would be the worst Christmas ever. Giving gifts to her enemy was so ironic. It would definitely give Losete the upper hand. Yikes!! She literally wanted to give a slap to Losete for her gift.

Enough was enough she wanted to exchange her slip. Like in any school there is a mean girl, and she has a sidekick, Losete (the mean girl) had a sidekick too, 'Alicia'. She had plans for exchanging her slip with Alicia / Sidekick / best friend of Losete.

But just as she was on her way to do that she thought, if she would be the one giving gifts to Losete she could arrange a truce. Which could be risky, but Losete really knew how to get a person on their nerves. Once she got a child expelled, just because that child was better than her in transformation and hence got better marks than her. Well only she knew how she pulled that off. She was evil and maybe a bit too extreme, which is precisely why it would be great if Hailey and Losete had a truce.

So she sat down and thought of gifts she could give to Losete, but how could she? There is so much noise and crowd. Just as she was on her way to her room she saw James running toward her in a hurry.

Hailey said, "Whoa dude, calm down over there. What happened?"

"Hailey I don't understand what's going on. Organio told me that Kyle's name is not on any slip!!" Replied James.

"You almost got me. There must be a mistake in the slip writing, so they must have missed Kyle. After all, there are so many students in Foxels. You shouldn't freak out so much! But I gotta ask did something happen to her, cause you look very worried." said Hailey.

"Well I don't know about her health, but yesterday she told me that she is making the slips. She can't just forget to write her own name and even that I had just gone to her room and I did NOT see her. In fact I have searched the whole school and I still did NOT find her!!" said James as a reply looking worried and stressed out. He had never been so stressed!!

"You even checked the restricted library? She takes the key from Miss Marina and goes there often to read historic, pre historic and many other kinds of books." said Hailey.

"Yes, yes I have checked the whole academy. Didn't you hear?" said James.

"Ok so what do we do?" asked Hailey.

"I guess we will relook again. I will be more calm with you around. Maybe I missed something." said James with a big sigh.

"What do we start with? We have no clue, no note and no letter. There is nothing left to check!" said Hailey, very-very confused.

"Well we will surely get our first clue from her room let's go come on."

Missing Slip

Hailey and James rushed to Kyle's room and found nothing, but nail paint. Just when Hailey looked at the nail paint she said "this nail paint is my mom's. She carries this nail paint everywhere, but how did this reach here."

"The only way this thing could have reached here is your mom. Was she hear?" said James.

"WHAT DO YOU MEAN!!" RETORTED HAILEY IN ANGER.

"Calm down okay. Getting angry won't get Kyle back."

"Sometimes you are supposed to understand the other person's feelings. All you care about is Kyle. It is as if you forgot about how I would sometimes feel. And I'm going. You do what YOU WANT!!! BYE" and so Hailey left the room and went dashing away.

James felt bad and understood what Hailey meant.

The next day he went to Hailey and said"I am so sorry. I shouldn't have blamed your mother. If I were in your shoes, I wouldn't have liked it either. I am so sorry, I really am." Said James.

"Fine I will come, but just for Kyle. Come on let's go" said Hailey and both of them went to her room again. This time they found a letter which said......

Dear daughter Haiely. Today I am telling you my true name which is Tempest Sharell. I support the Dark Magic. Your friend Kyle is with me and once We kill her we can add one drop of blood in a potion of mine, once my potion is complete we will pour the potion inside all the water pipes of the World Using Magic. Once every soul drinks the poison water they will be in our control and we will conquer the world. Once this plans succeeds we will conquer and rule over the universe. You have to meet me tomorrow at 12:00 pm in the Dungeons which are below you're rooms.

you're mother
Tempest

Hailey was shell shocked. She just could not believe and digest what she was reading. She read the message again and again. It was simply unbelievable. Finally, when her mind began to accept the content of the letter, her mind began to gravitate from utter disbelief, to shock, outrage and anger for her mom. She was **VERY** outraged.

With mixed feelings of sadness and anger, she remembered the loving cuddle of her mother, the loving way her mom gave her the courage she needed to go through anything she was afraid of, which calmed her down. She was so angry that she did not think about why a mom who was so loving, especially her mother who was the most caring person in the whole wide world would ever think of killing Kyle, poisoning the water pipes and controlling the world.

She literally felt crying as loud as possible. "She calls herself a mother, even after what all she has in her mind!! I hate her. Why would she do this?" wondered Hailey.

"Well what do you think?" asked James.

"Just to complete her potion she wants to kill Kyle and take away my BEST FRIEND. This is horrible. I can't believe it, I never knew anything about magic even though my mother is a magic evil person." said Hailey in a fit of rage and disbelief.

"What do we do now?" said James.

"Well first I want to know why she is up to all of this. We need to go to my home". And we'll search inside my house. I am sure the golden diary has something. I guess I just did not care to have a look at it. It is our last hope!!"Said Hailey

"What is the golden diary exactly?" said James.

"It was a diary which was in a drawer. Whenever I took it my mom would come running ...and forget about touching the diary... She wouldn't even allow me to see that diary. I am sure that diary has something that will help us a lot and give us the key and a chance to save Kyle." replied Hailey.

"But, how are we ever even supposed to go back?" said James.

"I don't know exactly." replied Hailey.

As the bell rang the two went to the assembly area.

"Good morning." Said Mowlem from the stage.

"Whatever we have to do we shall do. For now let's just go near the stage and listen to Professor Mowlem." Said Hailey.

"Ok." Replied James.

Mowlem said "Good morning children. Since it is Christmas we the Professors of Foxels Academy, announce that children will be allowed to return to their homes till Christmas, and may come back to Foxels any time between Christmas, though it is necessary to come back to this academy after Christmas break. The trains will leave tomorrow so the kids who wish to leave may start packing their bags."

The next morning Hailey and James seized this godsend opportunity and hopped into the train preparing to face a big war that was ahead of them waiting.

Once they reached Hailey's house they saw the golden diary. It was extremely well kept, neat, shining, very bright and embossed in gold. It indeed was a prized possession. Hailey and James could not think of any adjectives to describe its beauty. They were simply awestruck by the stunning impact it made on both of them. Hailey could barely get her eyes of that book.

"No wonder mom would clean this diary every 30 minutes!!!" said Hailey to James.

"You are so right. Clearly your mom loved that diary." said James.

"I can even see a logo," said Hailey.

"I think you should take a pic," said James.

"Ya... I better do that." said Hailey and took a picture of the logo.

"Now what?" said James?

"All I know is that this diary has some big secret inside it.... And now.....it is the time to discover the secret!!! Said Hailey ending the discussion.

Hook Hiekenstien and Tempest Sharell

When they opened the diary the first page flipped open and out floated the content...

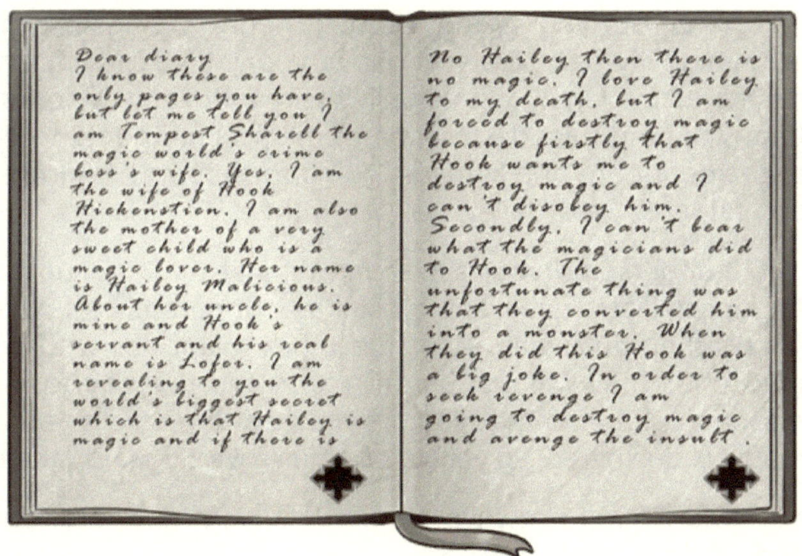

Dear diary
I know these are the only pages you have, but let me tell you I am Tempest Sharell the magic world's crime boss's wife. Yes, I am the wife of Hook Hiekenstien. I am also the mother of a very sweet child who is a magic lover. Her name is Hailey Malicious. About her uncle, he is mine and Hook's servant and his real name is Lofer. I am revealing to you the world's biggest secret which is that Hailey is magic and if there is

No Hailey then there is no magic. I love Hailey to my death, but I am forced to destroy magic because firstly that Hook wants me to destroy magic and I can't disobey him. Secondly, I can't bear what the magicians did to Hook. The unfortunate thing was that they converted him into a monster. When they did this Hook was a big joke. In order to seek revenge I am going to destroy magic and avenge the insult.

After reading this she was heartbroken and extremely curious. She had so many questions! The questions were never ending.

Those two pages had changed her life, she did not know what to do. Hailey thought her father was no more, but somehow all she knew was that magical people did something to him which made him a MONSTER!! Things were so very confusing. Hailey was magic!! How could Hailey believe this herself? She had to do so many things. Lastly, she couldn't believe her beloved uncle was a servant of **evil** or something......she could not rely on, or trust anyone except for herself. As she burst into tears and sobbed James tried to comfort her.

"Calm down Hailey. I know this is very hard to understand, but you need to know that you are very-very **powerful** and you have to do something, I mean at least something to save the world of magic!" said James.

"What are you asking me to do huh? Go against my mom and my dad! Are you out of your MIND? Magicians destroyed my family, it is actually their fault! There is no way I am stopping this...destruction of magic. I am going to go to the dungeons and I am just going to support my mother and father!!!" said Hailey, very *frustrated.*

"I understand your situation, but just think about this for once!! Few magicians must have done something to your father, but what about the other magicians who are innocent!! They will just be destroyed and that too for no reason at all!! Also that you are magic and magic is you. If magic is destroyed, so will you be destroyed!!!" said James.

"Okay I will not save magic by killing mom and dad and uncle though. I will save magic by doing something else. If my dad was magic's crime boss I'm pretty sure magic would have been destroyed long ago unless someone was out there who trapped him. Somehow my dad was able to escape, hence he came here and has targeted this place. If we research and find out how to trap him we can prison him in the place where he is meant to be trapped." said Hailey.

"You are right.....but where are we supposed to find such a particular book." said James inquisitively.

"SHOORKIE'S PANNEL LIBRARY. The library has 100 sections with each section with twenty nine cupboards and each cupboard containing 50 shelves and each shelf at the most accommodating 30 books. Oh! And ya this library is the world's biggest library, and luckily this Library is right next to our house!!!" said Hailey.

"Then let's go! What are we waiting for, come on!!" said James.

When they reached the library they saw this extremely old man, apparently the librarian who looked very *STUBBORN!!* The place was full of spooky spiders and spider webs!! Even though the place was very creepy and spooky there were thousands and thousands of books, making the place the biggest home of knowledge.

"Umm Mr. O could you tell me where is the book section on ancient history pertaining to magic?" asked Hailey.

"10 steps to the right and you will find the books on ancient history pertaining to magic" said Mr. O very strictly and very firmly.

"Thank you sir." said Hailey in a thankful and humble voice.

They went to the magic book section and the first thing they saw was the book.

James said "if this book is so easy to find then the magical world can be so easy to discover."

"You are right.....wait a second actually you can be

wrong." said Hailey.

"What do you mean?" said James.

"Ok." Then Hailey shouted "Mr O could you please come over here." said Hailey trying to prove her point.

"Coming." said O.

Hailey then picked up the book which they wanted to read.

When O came she said "O could you tell whether the book I am holding is fictional or nonfictional?"

"You are not even holding any book. Don't trick me again." Said O and stomped the way out.

James chuckled and now knew that the magical books were invisible for non magical people, they then started reading the book ⬚Adventures of Valusa Barnacles' and out flew the words before them which read...

I am Valusa barnacles,
The one who trapped hook Hiekenstien deep under the earth
in the dungeons.
The only way to imprison the monster also known as the crime boss of magic is to attack him right in the middle of his chest where he has a logo. The logo looks like this-

Hailey and James stopped right at the moment when they finished that page.

"Isn't that the logo which was on the golden diary?" said Hailey.

"I know. And as far as I understand your mother drew that logo." said James.

"Well we don't have time to ponder on these things, All I really care about is how to trap my dad in a dungeon;

"Well I have an idea in mind, but all we need to do for now to complete this utmost difficult task is to just keep this book in our bag." said James.

"But..." said Hailey.

"No but's and no if's, just action. Now COME ON!!" said James.

"Ok-ok." Said Hailey.

They packed their bags and caught the train the following night. The next morning they reached Foxels. Today was the day Hailey had to go inside the dungeons and meet her mother.

The Grand Entrance

It was half past 11. After 30 minutes Hailey had to go to the dungeons to see her parents who were half monsters. Hailey was very scared and so she went to James. When Transformation class was coming towards the end she asked him "You said you had a plan? Tell me the plan, I have to go into the dungeons after 30 minutes. My life is in supreme danger!!"

"Calm down Hailey. Firstly your life is very safe because you will meet your parents and they won't hurt you. They don't even know you are against them!! And secondly I have a plan, but I need you to go to the dungeons and just follow what is being said by your mom and dad if you want magic to be safe." Said James.

"But." Said Hailey.

"No time to waste. 10 minutes left. ***GO TO THE DUNGEONS!!*** " instructed James.

"Ok, but could you at least lead me till the dungeons?" asked Hailey.

"Fine let's go, come on." replied James and so they went towards the dungeons. They went into the corridors where the student rooms were. When they were roaming around in the corridors and had almost given up...they were lucky to finally spot a black arrow sticking right out of the old torn mat.

They pulled the mat over knowing it would give them a lead. And when they did pull the mat they were both shocked and surprised to see the same Logo springing out of the mat which was drawn in the golden diary.

"You should probably check that sign," said James.

"I do not have the golden diary at the moment. Had I had the diary, I could have easily matched to ascertain whether it is the same logo which was drawn in the golden diary." Said Hailey.

"No Dumbo, we can see the logo from the diary!! I had kept the Golden Diary inside your handbag." Fired James.

"Oh! Ok...um I am just checking." Said Hailey.

"Quick! No time to waste!!!" said James.

"Ok......aha!! I found the logo! It is exactly the same." Said Hailey.

"Hmmm... well I also kept Valusa Barnacle's book inside your handbag. You should check to find out how to get inside the dungeons of dungeons."

"Ok I guess......................there we go I found the book. And I have to open page 4. Ok here we go, page four is open. It says...

Chapter 2-Hiding place of Hook and Tempest

The place where Tempest Sharell and Hook sometimes hide is in the dungeons

Of Foxels academy. The main way to get to the dungeons is to get inside the corridors of the Student rooms of Foxels academy and search for a logo that is the same as the logo drawn in the middle of Hook's chest. You will find the logo somewhere in the student room's corridor. Then you have to stand right in the

Middle of the logo and the person who wants to enter the dungeons

Has to utter their name three times in their mind

And step backwards as fast as possible. Once they have

stepped back, the ground will open up like magical sesame and start cracking up.

A staircase will be seen. All that is left to do

now is to follow the staircase which will take the person and lead him to

The hiding place of Hook Hiekenstien and Tempest Sharell.

The place where their main stuff is kept is usually inside the dungeons of the dungeons.

To reach the dungeons of dungeons you have to follow a cave

Which is located in the dungeon of the student rooms.

"Come on, you read the book now, go in, and follow what your parents say, and lastly tell your mother to help us out. She is the only way we are winning from Hook. Ok?``said James looking very determined.

"Ok" said Hailey and did as per the instructions of James and the book.

When she said her name three times the ground started collapsing. James and Hailey were just too scared and so they ran backwards. The ground opened and they saw a staircase leading the two kids to the dungeons.

"From here you are alone. And remember to ask your mother about her helping us succeed in our plan." Said James.

"Ok, but could you please come with me?" asked Hailey.

"No" said James and pushed Hailey down right inside the dungeons. When she reached the dungeons all she could see was darkness and only darkness!!

"So you finally came down," said an unknown voice.

"The last time you said that was when you were dropping me till platform Alfa Century 2340. MOM!! You can change your voice, and your voice may trick anybody, but I can identify you in any voice or any look of yours. You don't need to change your voice." Said Hailey pretty sure that it was her mom who said this.

"Happy to know that you are at least talking to me!" said Tempest.

"Mom, you know I am not happy going against magic, and I know that father was embarrassed, but just because a few magicians made my dad a monster, you can't destroy life's of all the other magicians who are innocent." Said Hailey trying to tell her mother whatever her mother was doing was not at all good.

"How do you know about your dad... wait for a second, you read my golden diary, didn't you?" said her mother who had mixed feelings.

"I did... I was just so curious to know why you were a monster and so I thought that the golden diary surely had some big secret, that you were so secretive about it. Once I read the golden diary, I realised why you were a monster, and most importantly, I came to know about dad! You told me he died in a car crash! Talk about acting. You acted like you didn't know magic existed. I know you want to support him, but..." as soon as Hailey was going to ask her mom whether she could help her, a voice shouted

"So, this is my stupid and useless daughter?"

"Come out Hook!!" said Tempest.

As soon as Hook came out Hailey's mouth stuck wide open and she couldn't close it. This happened because Hook looked so scary with yellow eyes, red body and blue and black scars near his eyes. He was huge in size and looked like a nightmare.

A Grand Plan

"I promise not to disappoint you!!" said Hailey, very scared.

"I told you tempest, she made no use to us, when she knew about tempest and now that she knows about magic and most importantly—me, she will still be of NO use." Replied Hook and went away by creating cracks and holes on the ground of the dungeons below the student rooms.

"Ignore him Hailey, he is a bit harsh, but I am telling you he cares...he really does. Do you know he asks about you every day. Anyway, so.... what were you saying to me sweetie?" continued Hailey's mom Tempest.

"Nothing at all...just forgot what I had to say." Replied Hailey.

"Ok." said Tempest and then went away.

The reason Hailey had not asked this question was because, after looking at how dangerous her dad was and how powerful he could be, she did not have the guts to say anything against her dad.

The next morning, she started wondering about how she was going to save the magic world. She was even thinking about how powerful Hook would be! The same morning, she went back to James and told him everything that had happened. Now, James too knew that Hook was no joke. He knew that defeating him with Hailey was almost impossible, but he also knew that Hailey carried a power inside her that no body or soul could have ever carried. Suddenly his mind shot a great idea. He told Hailey his idea and so Hailey was also impressed.

The idea was that the only person who had ever trapped Hook was Valusa Barnacles, and so if they could somehow find Valusa they could have asked her how to trap Hook deep inside the ground. Hailey suggested looking at the book and searching for evidence of where or how to find Valusa Barnacles. "That is a good idea." Said James. When they opened the book, they saw a paper. The paper was half torn, consisting of some scribbled-up words. The two of them had never seen that before. James was surprised because he had been reading the book all the time, but he had never seen any kind of paper inside the book!! The paper said...

The fury of the sea,

Unknown too many,

Wrap it will in its shell,

The humble and the mighty,

Drown it will the deceitful and canny,

Solve this puzzle,

The answer lies in the seashore,

Where you will find me always apart,

Yet inseparable.

"So, I think we have to solve this riddle and end up with a result such as the dungeons which are placed deep under the ground. We could even end up finding Valusa Barnacles. This sounds so much fun! Come on let's do it!!" said Hailey after reading out the riddle from the torn page.

"I somehow agree and if we have to solve riddles like these to reach our desired destination, then lemme tell you I am **VERY** bad at solving riddles. You're kind of alone even if am next to you, because you will be solving the riddles." Replied James.

"Maybe we can start by searching the whole school at midnight sharp. You can search in half of the school while I can search the other half." Said Hailey.

"Ok. I like the plan. Let's do it girl!" said James and so the two kids went to their classes.

When all the first years had called it a day, Hailey and James went to their beds and when the clock struck midnight both of them met in the dining hall. Hailey said "it is twelve o'clock and we met on time. Part 1 is successful. Let's do part 2 which is searching the academy. You go right and I go left. Ok?"

"Ok. Come on let's go now." said James and so the two of them (Hailey and James) began their search. After a considerable period of time when Hailey and James found a bunch of nothing, they both sat down together and started thinking about the riddle. Hailey found out the answer and the answer was right! This is what happened:

"The riddle says the answer is in the sea shore. What is on the seashore? Aha! On the seashore there are sea shells. And the shells are apart from the sea, but they are still related to the sea. I think I just got the answer to the riddle." Said Hailey to herself, and rushed to James' room. Then she took out a shell which she had mistakenly picked up from the ground while the fff tournament was going on.

When she looked at the shell carefully she found a paper that had the next riddle.

The next riddle said-

Now you have to find a tunnel,

Take your time don't be in a hustle,

If you miss a single detail,

You will have to start,

From the beginning of this way.

"Great, now we have to find a tunnel." Said James. Though he was happy he found the next riddle he did not like the idea of searching for a tunnel because after searching half the academy his legs were tired and full of pain. Clearly, he was VERY tired to do anything.

"I don't want to rush up with your feelings, but we cannot afford to waste time so we need to hurry and search for Kyle because Hook is very-very powerful and scary." Said Hailey and then they started their search. When they could not find a result, they sat near the river that was inside the boundaries of Foxels academy desperately searching for a lead. As they thought and thought and thought it was nearly dawn. Suddenly they heard a sound that broke the early morning silence. The sound was absurd though Hailey could identify the sound. The sound was of a rock. The sound was coming because James was throwing pebbles in the river out of frustration at having to answer the riddle. "Why are the rocks making such an absurd sound?" asked Hailey to James.

"I guess they are hitting something hard that is under the water." Replied James.

"Hmmmmm...." said both of them and there was a minute of silence.

"What would have been the material that hit the rock?" asked Hailey to James.

"Maybe ... just ... maybe it was a tunnel..." replied James.

"Should we go and check?" said Hailey.

"Good idea, let's do It." said James and they went under water. When they went under water they saw an enormous cave which was guarded by a one-eyed octopus. When James and Hailey went next to him they felt very nice because the one-eyed octopus was super friendly to them and somehow knew that Hailey and James were very humble and mighty. With the permission of Roockie (the one-eyed octopus) the two kids entered the tunnel. Before going inside, Roockie gave Hailey and James a red belt that allowed them to talk, breathe and live inside the sea.

The tunnel was gigantic and it had thorns sticking out of its top.

When the tunnel was about to end a very strong, windy and cold waves came over. It was so strong that it ambushed Hailey and James and they were unable to handle themselves. When the strong wave stopped James found a paper stuck right behind Hailey's back. When James took out the paper he saw the next riddle in place. "We found the next riddle! We found the next riddle! Yaaaaaay!!" shouted James. He was very happy to find the next riddle and so he took out the paper which was stuck behind Hailey. Hailey was equally happy. They swam back to the end and found a huge tunnel kind of a room. The room was very massive and colossal. "What is the next riddle exactly?" asked Hailey to James. "The next riddle says:

"The place where you stand,

Has a treasure of stories,

The place is such, it will solve this path,

Of riddles and queries."

"So... what place has a treasure of stories?" asked James to Hailey.

"This is such an easy riddle I can't understand why you don't get it." said Hailey after a **biiiiiiiiig** and **IRRITATING** sigh.

"I don't understand MEANS I don't understand. Just tell the answer because we are in a BIG HURRY!" said James with the impatience clearly visible in his face.

"Well if I am correct then the answer should probably be a library." Said Hailey.

"Where would be the library? This infinitely long tunnel seems never ending." replied James.

"Well, searching this whole tunnel might be the last thing we do, but I am stipulating to you: we are going to find this library." Said Hailey.

"Fine let's begin with the search." Replied Hailey and so the kids began another adventure.

After a considerable period of time they ultimately found the library. The tunnel was pulchritudinous in its own way, but Hailey noticed that the library was equally pulchritudinous as the tunnel. The library was solid gold from the outside. From the inside it was even better because it was made up of diamonds. The diamonds were glamorous and they shone as bright as a spangle. Inside the library stood a neatly dressed woman who wore a blue frock. Her name was Lisa Phylon and she was extremely beautiful. Her eyeballs shone like diamonds, hair was untangled and straight. She even had fringes and her hair was as deep as the sea. Her lips were blood red. She had the cleanest skin of all. Her shoes were made of glass. She was thin and had a medium height. And lastly her skin was as gentle as a petal.

She had a similar sister who was exactly the opposite of her. Her hair was tangled and they were super curly. Her shoes had dust on them. Her lips had turned like an old flower that is dead and she wore round and big spectacles. She had mud on her dress and her skin was dirty. She wore loose pants and a light blue t-shirt. Her name was Jacksie Phylon. Even though the two twins were completely opposite, two of them had one thing in common which was their eyeballs. Both of them had eyeballs that shone like diamonds. James lost himself for a minute.

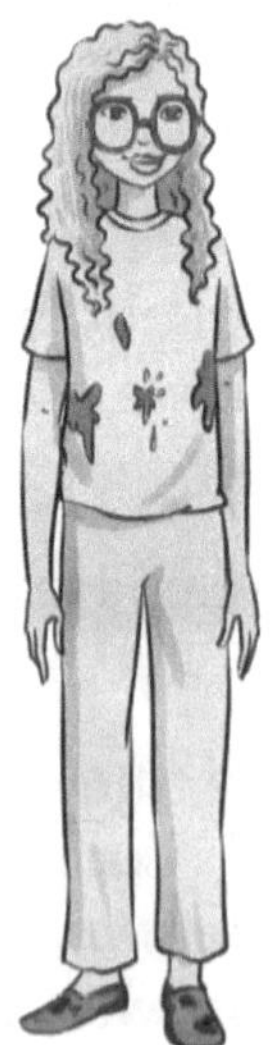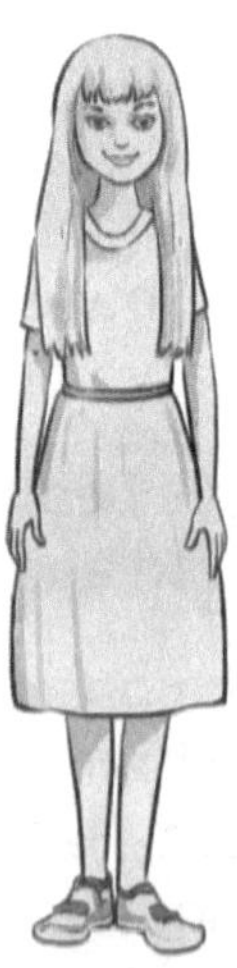

What all was happening around James and Hailey was unbelievable. It was the shine in the diamond like eyes of the sisters which bought both James and Hailey back to their senses. When they were done with day-dreaming they told the two girls what had happened.

"Well ya two have come to the right place. We girls know everything about Albatraz prison." said Jacksie.

"Albatraz prison? What is that? I mean I know it is a prison, but......what's Albatraz for?" said Hailey.

"Well ya see Albatraz is the only prison that has the power to imprison Hook Hiekenstien. I' m sure you both know about this prison. The riddles and the book must have given you the acknowledgement of the prison that imprisons Hook Hiekenstien. The prison deep in earth? Don't ya know?" replied Jacksie.

"Who is Albatraz?" Hailey asked.

"Well da ya know who Valusa Barnacles is?" said Jacksie.

"Yeah we do. She was the one who imprisoned Hook Hiekenstien. She even has a book. The book is more like a guide or so." James replied.

"I sure am glad that you both know about Valusa. She is my BFF. Her nickname was Alba and her father's name was Traz, hence we named the prison Albatraz. We named the Albatraz Prison in their name because those people imprisoned Hook 1000 years ago. As you know he has now escaped from prison.'' Jacksie.

"Ok so I am kind of understanding the situation. Not to mention it is super absurd, but no matter what, I don't understand one thing and that is - why did the last riddle lead us over here to this library?" said Hailey.

"Well you see we guard the prison. It is placed under the science lab which is beneath this library. The keys are with me and I will take you to the prison. We have to do things very quickly because there are many things to do, but hardly any time to do them. Once I show you the prison you two could imprison Hook by using the plan you two have in mind." Said Lisa.

"We have to go deeper. I mean seriously...first, we went to a tunnel that leads us to a place that is a dungeon. Then we have to go to a science lab that is beneath this dungeon to reach the prison that is beneath the science lab. Next up you two sisters will tell me that I have to spend my whole life in a dungeon like you two!" Said James.

"Well ya see we need to keep the prison safe and confidential so just shut up and first tell me your plan." Said Jacksie.

"We don't exactly have......um a plan" said Hailey.

"Not something I like, but...... as I am getting to know you...I was ready for this answer." Replied Jacksie.

"So, what do we do now?" said Hailey.

"Follow me down till the prison and on the way, Jacksie will tell you how you two will prison Hook." Said Lisa.

"Ok." Said James and Hailey.

As they walked Hailey felt that she should tell Jacksie that her father was Hook. Ultimately, she thought that telling Jacksie would be the best thing to do, but when she went to Jacksie, Jacksie started telling the two of them what would be the way they could imprison Hook. Hailey sighed and thought that she would announce this piece of information later.

The plan looked somewhat like this-

"So, Hook will be on the southern island on 9th of December and not in dungeons of dungeons probably because it will be the day when he was prisoned and he is smart enough to think that Valusa might come to prison him in the dungeons of dungeons again.

According to my secret spies and Lisa's secret cameras, he should be on the southern islands. Our friend general Iro will be on the Eastern Island and we will tell him to go and take all the battle equipment from the underground basement also known as UB through the tele-message, an invention of my sister.

The tele-message records the message that you want to send and then asks who to send the message to. Once you tell the tele-message who to send the message to, the tele-message records your answer and then it goes to that person at the speed of light and that's how it delivers the desired message to the right person.

So, after receiving a message informing him about the present situation and how he can help us, when he will take the battle equipment. Me, Lisa, James and you will go to Hook and distract him until General Iro is ready with the battle equipment. Then......" said Jacksie who was not able to complete her sentence.

"Wait you just now said that me, Lisa, James and you will go to Hook and distract him, but, how will we? My fath.... I mean Hook is too strong. We can't do this on our own." Said Hailey.

"Oh! Of - course we won't do it on our own. Valusa will help us as she will too, leave from her island when we do, so that Valusa reaches the southern island at the same time as us. Also, we will be having a green emerald that will make us super tiny which will make it hard for Hook to see us." Replied Jacksie.

"If Valusa will be there then why do we need to go...... or for that fact why does anyone ever have to go? She can imprison Hook anytime she wants. After all she was the one who imprisoned him the first time." Said Hailey.

"Valusa has lost her powers because she gave them all to the green emerald which was later spoiled by Tempest Sharell, a friend who has special powers. Now the only power the emerald is left with is a power that makes one super tiny." Said Jacksie.

"Ok weird, but it is best not to get back into the history since the past is CONFUSING. VERY-VERY CONFUSING. Just tell us your plan and we'll follow it." Said Hailey with a sigh.

"Thank you, where was I now? Ya so when me, Lisa, James and you go to Hook and distract him, General Iro will be ready with his army and battle equipment. Then we will take Hook in the middle of the sea using all the powers that Valusa still has. When we go to the middle of the sea General Iro will go to the middle of the sea using the battle equipment. Once Hook and IRO are face to face then we will get on Iro's battle ships and the battle will begin. The Monstrous Sea is the best option and strategy in defeating Hook. Our plan will definitely work because the Monstrous Sea has waves as high as mountains and only we can face them because of our amazing battle tools. I am so confident about our plan. It will totally rock." Said Jacksie completing her plan.

Hailey thought that right now telling Jacksie that Hook is her dad would be the best thing to do.

"Um.... Jacksie I wish to tell you um...... that...... that...... Hook is my fath..." said Hailey not able to complete her sentence.

"We are here. Albatraz prison is in front of your eyes." Interrupted Lisa.

"Yeah, so what were you saying about Hook?" asked Jacksie.

"Nothing......... it was nothing." Said Hailey feeling that it would be prudent to disclose this piece of information later, as she felt uncomfortable in disclosing that telling her father was a monster who tried to destroy the world of magic.

Albatraz prison was HUGE. It was made of steel and diamond. It had the 'Saistristal' on it which was one of the most beautiful diamonds ever found.

"This is the Saistristal diamond, one of the most beautiful, powerful, large and destructive diamonds of all. This is the only unique piece that can now be the end of Hook only if Hook has a child.

Well we might win through the plan I told ya gals before, but this diamond has to be used if our plan......well does not work. Coming back to the diamond. The diamond consists of a plethora of magic. Whoever dares to touch this diamond dies. None of this might make sense to you so listen to this tale.

In 1985 when Hook had taken over Masashue, the first country ever, the sultan of the land told everybody to start worshipping the fire, water, air, land, forests and mystical creatures for three days. This was because the mighty evil Hook, Tempest and Loafer had taken over the land. When the people worshipped the fire, water, air, land, forests and mystical creatures, the gods were happy and gave birth to Valusa to stop Hook. Later on, she defeated Hook, but even the gods knew that Valusa had to die one day, and Hook might escape from the Albatraz prison. They feared he would be unstoppable if Valusa weren't there so they made a diamond that was 10 times stronger than her. It was very-very powerful. It is said that only the child of Hook and Tempest can save the day, because there is a saying that only the child of two powers like Tempest and Hook will have enough magic to touch the diamond.

So when Tempest and Hook have a child, the child will consist of all their powers combined, but even if they have a child, we are not sure whether they will help, I mean that person is **THEIR** child." said Jacksie.

"Sheesh! Where do you get all that information from?" said James.

"Well we don't have time to tell. We need to find work on other machines for the war!" said Jacksie, all angry.

"Um...I guess maybe I have something to tell." Said Hailey with a sigh.

"Uh! How many things can a person ask at once!" said Jacksie, getting more annoyed.

"Um, you probably won't believe me, but um I um...well I am Hook's daughter and it is the truth, you can even ask James if you want to, and I can prove it by holding Saistristal diamond. Also, I am really sorry for not informing you guys before. I was a bit shy, I have just met you, you know." Said Hailey anticipating a negative response.

The two sisters looked at each and then Jacksie came and said "look ya little sugercue it is perfectly ok to be shy and admit this, though it would have been more helpful if you would have told this information to us before, but it is great to know this information and you a little-bittle more. We are just glad you admitted it.

Now we can have a better plan with the help of the diamond. We must keep you safe, as I said the diamond is powerful and so it will protect you, but we shouldn't take chances. And trust me, the new plan will be very simple, now that we have the diamond."

"Thanks for believing in me, I will do as you say." Then Hailey went to pick the diamond.

When she did a very bright light shone and she was turned into a living dream. Her lips were as red as roses, her dress changed into something gorgeous, her eyes were like diamonds, her skin shone as bright as the sun and just in one look it was easy to notice that her skin was as soft as a petal. She was wearing a blue top with a heart and jeans. James, Lisa and even Jacksie were stunned. The diamond was shining brighter than ever.

"There is no time to waste, our new plan is simple. We will sneak into Hook's hiding place which will be the southern island in the night. Then Hailey will sneak into Hook's bedroom and keep the diamond on Hook's chest, exactly where his power sign is.

But in order to reach Hook we must defeat Tempest who will be wide awake, so we will be there for help, but Hailey by herself has to keep the diamond out of Tempest's sight and then put the diamond on Hook's power sign. To go through Tempest, you shall tell her that you have come here to defeat magical people, and then go according to this plan and keep the diamond on Hook's chest." completed Lisa.

"Clear" said James, Jacksie and Hailey and so they all waited for the middle of the night, to win the fight.

On The Rescue

It was 9 pm, the moment Hailey was desperately waiting for. The whole dungeon was silent. The sea waves could be heard and so could the clock's tick-tock breaking the tranquil silence in between. If Hailey were successful in her plan she would become the hero of the magical world, but if not well then it means the end of the WORLD!

"Let's go to the southern side where Hook is hiding, but it is not so close. It will even take time if we use my TSM (The TSM is a gadget designed by Lisa. It is a mode of transportation. It is extremely fast. It can cover 15 km per minute.)." said Lisa.

"Right, we should probably move," said Hailey.

"Ok then. Sit on the TSM" Said Lisa.

Everybody sat on the machine and they were on the rescue.

It was cold and foggy outside the dungeons. After some time, they reached the southern island. Unexpectedly they saw a whole bunch of guards.

"What do we do now?" said Hailey.

"I know a sleep spell and I tried it on my mother. It will work here too, I assume." Said James.

"Worth a shot," said Jacksie.

"Admaskio lajuria" said James and waved his wand towards the guards.

Zzz slept the guards and fell into deep-deep sleep. Once the guards were asleep they went through the bushes.

"Now we are at the entrance gate door, you have to be on your own for the rest of the plan. Good luck" said Lisa.

"Thanks. I'll try my best not to freak-out." Replied Hailey.

"Good luck," said James.

Hailey hugged her friends and opened the door. When she looked back she saw that James, Lisa and Jacksie were gone, so she continued. She hid the diamond in her pocket and went on. The whole palace was silent. As she continued she saw Tempest, her mother. She tried to ignore her mother, but Tempest asked

"Why are you here and how did you know about this place? According to my letter I had only told you about the dungeons, not about the southern island's palace. Also, how did you cross the sea, and only come here today, that too at night?"

"Um actually I was here through a spell. And I used a spell to travel till here and I read some books about father so I knew that today is going to be a war day hence, maybe dad could need my help, for fighting to Valusa Barnacles." Said Hailey hoping Tempest would believe her.

"Well.......if you say so. Go in." replied Tempest with a sigh, never thinking that her own daughter was about to betray her.

Hailey didn't have great plans. She was so freaked out

by the creepy look of the palace. She just thought of simply keeping the diamond on Hook's chest and then running out, in case the diamond destroyed Hook along with the palace. So, she went to Hook's room which was pitch dark, she quickly kept the diamond on Hook's chest and then ran....and BOOOOM the castle was destroyed! It was done. There was smoke all around. Internally she felt that she should not have killed her own dad, but she even knew that if she did not kill Hook, Hook would kill her and the world of magic. Suddenly she got flashbacks of when she was a baby. She didn't exactly remember how her dad looked, but it made her feel guilty. She missed the only chance to be with her family.

"I did it...I killed my" Hailey said interrupted by Tempest.

"Your own father and my husband?" said Tempest interrupting Hailey.

"Tempest... you.... here?" asked Hailey.

"Yes, it is me! And you thought you had defeated me? I am immortal and diamond was the only enemy of me and now it is lost in the broken pieces of my lovely palace. Just because I am your mother doesn't mean that I will not destroy GOOD MAGIC and mag...." said Tempest, unable to complete her sentence.

"ATTACK!" shouted Jacksie interrupting Tempest.

A whole army came running towards the island.

"General Iro? Jacksie? James? Lisa? And Kyle!! What... how..." said Hailey, seeing her friends, General Iro and Kyle!

Hailey went running towards her friend. She went to them and the five friends had a very TIGHT group hug, but there was no time to waste as the war had started.

"ATTACK!" shouted Tempest and an army of Goblins came in front of Hailey, her friends and General Iro. The Goblins were all green and grody. Saliva was dripping out of their rather small mouths. Their teeth were as sharp as needles and they were wearing torn clothes that were brown in color.

The war was going to be furious by the looks of it.

When both sides commanded their army to attack, the war started. The war and its intensity was so furious it never seemed to end so Hailey thought if she could find the Saistristal diamond (which was lost somewhere in the broken pieces of the palace) she would be able to destroy Tempest but, how could she? She was not even sure whether the Saistristal diamond was in a condition good enough to be used. Its condition was important because it defined how much power it had.

Then she thought that finding the Saistristal diamond would take a lot of time and even if they found the diamond it would be useless, firstly because the goblin army commanded by Tempest would have already won and secondly, because it would obviously would not be as powerful as it was before as it could have suffered a lot of damage while destroying Hook. Then suddenly something struck her mind, she thought that she **_was_** magic, and way more powerful than her parents. Couldn't she use her own powers?? All she knew was that, going to Valusa and finally meeting her would make her feel better as Valusa Barnacles knew everything, she thought she could help Hailey use her own magic. She went to Jacksie who was helping Lisa bring her machines for the war.

She told Jacksie her plan, but Jacksie said that Valusa was destroyed along with the palace as she was supposed to meet you in the palace. The thing is that the blast happened just when she was inside the palace trying to come to you. It is indeed the most tragic thing that could ever happen, but it is just true.

She even told Hailey that trying to help Lisa bring war machines would be a better plan. Hailey wasn't satisfied, but still agreed. The goblins were taking over. Iro's army was almost finished. Then something happened which turned out to be the reason for good's victory against bad. That something was when Kyle was hit by Tempest's scepter. Hailey turned red. There was silence and then Hailey flew in the sky with her eyes all white. And she spread a light so bright it destroyed the whole army of goblins.

Her mother, Tempest shouted "NOOOOOOOOOOOOOOO!" as she and her goblin army was DESTROYED. Hailey landed on the ground. There was not a single sound except the wind whooshing and swooshing. The intensity and the power of her magic within generated so much energy that it destroyed the enemy. Gradually Hailey began to regain her original self.

"It's over," said Hailey with a sigh of relief.

Not A Goodbye After All

It was one week after the war.

Hailey, James, Lisa and Jacksie were waiting outside the Telescoth hospital. Kyle, came out as fit as a fiddle and Hailey ran towards her and hugged her as tight as possible.

"I guess this is goodbye." said Jacksie. Who was almost in tears from what had happened.

"It is not a goodbye after all." Said Tentus Organio the headmaster of the school.

"What do you mean Mr. Organio?" asked Lisa.

"What I mean is that you and your sister can't study here, but you all can be here to help all the teachers in here and develop. Like Lisa can be the perfect one for the development of our school, and Jacksie knows so much about history as Hailey told.

I think she can talk about the history of magic in assemblies. Like talking about an historical legend or artifact or anything that Jacksie thinks should be told to the students of this school. This is a suggestion if you don't agree then you must do what you want. It is your wish." Said Mr. Organio

"We will be ***MOST HONORED TO DO SO*** Mr. Organio"

shouted Jacksie with excitement.

"J (Jacksie) is right, we would be honored." Said Lisa.

"Very well then. We have a deal. See you in school Lisa and Jacksie it was a pleasure to meet you." Replied Organio.

"And as for Hailey and Kyle and James, well; come to my office today at 5:00." Said Organio.

Later at school Hailey was thanked by every teacher and student, even Losete! It was the last day of school and practically the best.

At 5:00 when Hailey Kyle and James went to headmaster Tentus Organio he said "I want to thank you for saving the world of magic. This new secret that has been unlocked about Ms. Hailey Malicious, is a very big advantage for Foxels. It is indeed a delight for all of us to know she has defeated Hook, Tempest and their goblin army. This epic event is simply unbelievable and to show how thankful we are for this extraordinary action by Hailey we hereby announce that Hailey will be known as the saviour of magic. We give James, Jacksie, Lisa and Kyle, the reward of bravery and announce them as heroes of the magical world.

Regards,

Horehoof, seventh lord of magic."

That perhaps was a thank you letter from the lords of magic, written by my dearest friend Horehoof, who also happens to be one of the seven lords of magic. Now I would want to say I thank you all so-so much for saving this school Hailey, Kyle and James." Completed Organio.

"Thank you, headmaster, I couldn't be more honored and thankful." Said Hailey.

"Yes headmaster" said Kyle and James.

"Give this reward to Jacksie and Lisa." Said Organio handing over a letter.

"Ok headmaster." Said Hailey and left the office with her friends.

The next week the first years had to go home again and then come back in 3 months for their second year at Foxels academy, to start another new adventure and experience magic. Hailey was excited and eagerly looking forward to next year.

Everyone had left the school and all the students along with the teachers were bidding goodbye. After the students left something happened that prevented all the professors from even taking a step out of the school......

HAILEY AT FOXELS ACADEMY

Hailey Malicious is a normal girl until she receives a letter from Foxels academy school of magic. She goes to the magical school and meets Kyle and James who become her two best friends. But things change when Kyle goes missing. When Hailey and James go on a path to find Kyle they unlock so many secrets! Everything becomes very difficult as the evil Hook is trying to destroy the world of magic. Now it is up to Hailey to not only save her friend, but even save the world of magic! Read this book and find out about the thrilling and amazing adventures of Hailey and her friends.

GJ

9 789390 640225